E
VES

Vesey, A.

Duncan's tree house.

$18.95

23706

DATE			

DUNCAN'S TREE HOUSE

DUNCAN'S TREE HOUSE

by Amanda Vesey

Carolrhoda Books, Inc./Minneapolis

For Anna, Milly, and Johnnie

This edition published 1993 by Carolrhoda Books, Inc.

First published 1992 by HarperCollins, London
Copyright © 1992 by Amanda Vesey

Library of Congress Cataloging-in-Publication Data

Vesey, A.
    Duncan's Tree House / Amanda Vesey.
    p.   cm.
    Summary: Duncan experiences the worst night of his life
when he decides to stay overnight in his new tree house.
    ISBN 0-87614-784-8
    [1. Tree Houses–Fiction. 2. Night–Fiction.] I. Title.
PZ7.V6138Dv   1993
[E]–dc20   92-37334
                                                    CIP
                                                     AC

Manufactured in the United States of America

1 2 3 4 5 6 98 97 96 95 94 93

On Duncan's birthday, his parents gave him a tree house.
Duncan's father was a builder. He had made the tree
house in his workshop, and he had put it up the night
before Duncan's birthday, when Duncan was asleep.
It was a complete surprise to Duncan.

Inside the tree house was a bed and a rug and a table and a chair and a shelf with cups and plates on it. There was a bookcase and a tin box for keeping things in. The window had real glass in it, and it opened and shut.

Duncan leaned out of the window and waved to his parents in the yard below.

"Thank you!" yelled Duncan.

"I'll put up a sign so that everyone will know whose house it is," said Duncan.

He carved DUNCAN'S TREE HOUSE with his penknife on a piece of wood, and he painted it.

Then he nailed it to the handrail outside his front door.

Duncan spent most of his time in the tree house.

He put posters up on the walls.

He put toys in the tin box
and books in the bookcase.

He played with his monsters,
his space shuttle, and his
remote control moon buggy.

He didn't have to pick them up
when he was through.

Sometimes his mother made him a picnic lunch so that he could stay in the tree house all day.

He could play his radio as loud as he liked, and there was no one to tell him to turn the music down…

…but if he wanted a nice, restful silence, there was no one to disturb him, either.

Sometimes Duncan
watched the birds
and squirrels through
his father's binoculars.
When he didn't
know the names of the
birds, he looked them
up in his bird book.

Sometimes he drew pictures of the view from the tree. He could watch the boats on the river, the tractors in the fields, and a neighbor hanging out the wash.

One day, Duncan had an idea.

"I want to spend a night in the tree house," said Duncan.

His parents weren't sure about this.

"Are you sure that's a good idea, Duncan?" asked his father.

"Are you sure you won't be lonely all by yourself?" asked his mother.

Duncan was sure.

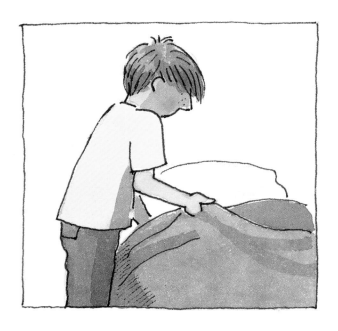

Duncan put extra blankets
on the bed.

He borrowed a big flashlight
from his father and checked
the batteries in his pocket
flashlight.

He packed a midnight feast in
case he got hungry in the night.

He couldn't wait for bedtime.

"I'm leaving," said Duncan after supper.
His mother gave him some cocoa and a hot water bottle.

"Take Buster with you," said his mother.
"Buster is big and brave. You'll feel safer
with him."

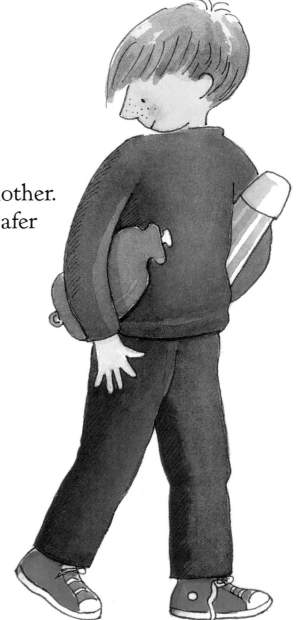

Buster was fat and not used to ladders. Duncan coaxed and wheedled and pushed and pulled. In the end he had to heave him up, step by step.

Duncan put on his pajamas and his
bathrobe. There wasn't any running water
at the tree house so he didn't have to brush
his teeth or wash.
He sat outside his front door and
read a book until it grew dark.

"Time for bed," said Duncan.

He switched on the flashlight. It was a powerful flashlight, but the light didn't reach into the corners. Tall, black shadows sprang up and danced across the room.

"We'll feel cozier in bed," said Duncan.

The bed faced the window. There were no curtains, and it was inky black outside.

"Suppose something horrible climbs up the ladder and peers through the window," thought Duncan. "Something terrible with yellow eyes and big pointed teeth..."

Crash! Something thumped against the windowpane.

Duncan put his head under the covers.

It was only a moth, attracted by the light.

When he fell asleep, Duncan had a nightmare about wolves.
"Yowl! Wail! Yelp!" howled the wolves as they chased
him through a forest.

Duncan woke up, but the howling didn't stop.
It was Buster who was howling. He was
scratching at the door. Buster wanted to go out.

Getting a fat dog up a ladder in daylight is one thing.
Getting a fat dog down a ladder in the dark while carrying
a flashlight is another.

When they reached the ground, Buster waddled off
into the darkness.

"Come back, Buster!" cried Duncan.

Come back! Come back! Duncan's voice echoed through
the trees as he stumbled through the undergrowth. Black
clouds scudded across the moon. The night was alive
with hootings and screechings and rustlings. A great
white owl swooped out of the shadows. Branches clawed
at Duncan; brambles tore his clothes.

Something was moving through the bushes. A grunting Something, a huge, heavily breathing Something, snapping twigs as it came nearer. And nearer…

Duncan fled back toward the tree house. The Something followed close behind him.

Crash! Duncan stumbled in the darkness and landed face down in a bramble patch, dropping his flashlight.

"Help!" cried Duncan as the Something landed on top of him.

It was Buster.

*   *   *   *

The tree house felt welcoming and safe. Duncan sat up in bed and ate a bar of chocolate.

"You don't deserve any chocolate," Duncan told Buster. But he gave him a piece anyway.

Crack! There was a great flash of lightning. Boom! Boom! Thunder rolled overhead. Then came the steady hiss of rain.

The rain fell harder and harder. It lashed against the window and drummed on the roof. The tree house shook and shuddered with every thunderclap.

Buster was afraid of thunderstorms. He clung to Duncan while the storm raged over the tree house.

"This is the worst night of my entire life," said Duncan.

When Duncan awoke, the sun was streaming through
the window. The birds in the tree were singing and
bickering and calling to each other.

"Wake up!" said Duncan. "It's a beautiful morning."

Duncan and Buster sat outside the front door and
shared the midnight feast.

Duncan watched a fisherman on the riverbank and the swallows swooping over the water. A breeze rustled the leaves of the tree. There was a smell of damp earth, and everything looked fresh and sparkling after the rain.

"Breakfast time, Duncan!"
It was his mother, calling from the foot of the ladder.
"Did you have a good night in your tree house?"

"Terrific," said Duncan.